MAIN LIBRARY

Running 50 vs. 100 Strides
(The Story of "One Who Ran 50 Steps Laughs at One Who Ran a 100 Steps)

五十步笑百步（半斤八兩）

WINDSOR PUBLIC LIBRARY

從前，有一個國家，常常和別國打仗。這個國家的軍隊裏，有兩個士兵，一個叫張武勝，一個叫李思標。他們倆很不喜歡打仗，可是除了當兵，他們也不會做別的事，只好當一天算一天了！

Long ago, there was a nation that constantly fought with other nations. In this nation's military, there were two unusual soldiers. One of them was called Zhang Wusheng, and the other was called Lee Sebiao. Neither enjoyed warfare. Yet, since they didn't know any other trade or craft, they remained in the military. So, they were forced to live from day to day.

One day, it was time for battle again. "Rm-pa-pa-pa-pum!" sounded the battle drums. Zhang Wusheng and Lee Sebiao looked at each other nervously.

有一天，又要作戰了！「
鼕！鼕！鼕！」戰鼓響了起
來！張武勝和李思標很緊張
的互相望了一望。

The commander yelled, "Charge!" And the soldiers yelled, "Charge! Charge!" Heading toward enemy territory, they took their weapons and fought for their lives.

Zhang Wusheng and Lee Sebiao were in front at first, but as they continued, they started to lag behind!

指揮官一聲:「上!」「衝啊!衝啊!」士兵們拿著武器,拼命往敵人的陣地攻進去。

張武勝和李思標本來排在前頭,跑著跑著卻落後了!

A while later, as the two nations continued the battle, the enemy troops started drawing nearer and nearer. Finally, Zhang and Lee's nation was defeated. Zhang Wusheng and Lee Sebiao saw that they were in trouble. Immediately throwing away their helmets and armor, they ran for their lives.

才沒多久,前面的敵人反而攻了過來。「殺!殺!」兩個軍隊打打殺殺。結果,張武勝這一邊的軍隊敗了下來。張武勝和李思標一看情形不對,馬上丟掉盔甲,飛快的逃命。

They ran and ran, farther and farther.

The two of them finally escaped to a safe place! Since Zhang Wusheng's legs were long, he could run faster than Lee Sebiao.

Gasping for air, Lee Sebiao yelled back, "Don't run anymore! Zhang Wusheng, the enemy can't catch us now! You're so afraid of death! Running away so quickly, what kind of hero are you?"

跑、跑、跑！跑、跑、跑！

他們倆終於逃到安全地帶了！張武勝腿長，比李思標跑得快了一些。

李思標在後面上氣不接下氣的喊道：「別跑了！張武勝，敵人追不上我們！你真是怕死啊！逃得這麼快，算什麼英雄好漢！」

Lee Sebiao's teasing caused Zhang Wusheng's face to immediately turn bright red.

Overhearing Lee Sebiao's comments, a farmer nearby started laughing and said, "What a joke! What's the difference between running away fifty steps and running away a hundred steps? Aren't you both running away? Six of one and half dozen of the other. You're both cowards!"

Immediately, Lee Sebiao's face also turned beet red. Obviously, Lee was also afraid of dying. How could he make fun of someone else?

張武勝被李思標一說，臉立刻紅了起來。

旁邊一個農夫聽到李思標的話，忍不住笑起來，說：「這可真是個笑話哇！逃五十步和逃一百步，有什麼不一樣呢？不都一樣是逃走嗎？一個半斤，一個八兩，都是膽小鬼！」

這下，李思標也臉紅了，原來他自己也是怕死的人，還笑別人怕死哩！

Parental Guide

After finishing reading the above story, you can let your children judge. Questions such as "What was wrong with Lee Sebiao laughing at someone else's behavior?" and "Why would Lee Sebiao laugh at his friend Zhang Wusheng?" will develop children's ability to distinguish right from wrong. On a daily basis, children may face the same situation as did Lee Sebiao. They blame others for the mistakes that they themselves have done. If that happens, remind them of the above story. Children can easily understand the irony and inappropriateness of "the kettle calling the pot black." Perhaps then they will learn not to reproach others for the very fault that they themselves possess.

Atu Yanks the Rice Seedlings
(The Story of "Pulling up the Seedlings to Make Them Grow Faster")

阿塗拔秧苗（揠苗助長）

Long ago, there was a person named Atu, who had a quick temper. No matter what he did, he was always impatient. He was only concerned about getting rid of the work as fast as possible. Because of this problem, he never learned any skills. Fortunately, his family had a plot of land. So, his father had him help in the fields.

從前，有一個人，名叫阿塗。他是個急性子，無論做什麼事，都毛毛躁躁的，恨不得趕快就做好。就因為這個毛病所以一直學不到一門手藝。幸好，他家裏還有塊田，他的爸爸就讓他在家裏幫忙種田。

Spring came! Atu and his father went to the fields to plant rice seedlings. Atu's father taught him to plant each one by one in the field. As Atu planted, he mumbled, "Darn! Planting like this is too slow! With such a big field, when will we ever finish?"

His father cautioned him, "Atu, you shouldn't be so rash. Stop being so impatient. Otherwise, you won't learn how to farm as well."

Atu pouted and was silent. It was not easy, but he persisted and finished planting the rice seedlings with his father.

春天來了！阿塗和爸爸到田裏插秧。爸爸教阿塗把秧苗一撮一撮插在田裏，阿塗一邊插，一邊嘀咕：「唉呀！這樣插太慢了，這一大片田，什麼時候才插得完呢？」

爸爸勸他說：「阿塗，你這急性子，要改一改了，不然，你連種田都學不會的。」

阿塗噘著嘴不說話，勉強耐著性子，跟爸爸，一起把秧插完。

A few days later, Atu's father told him to go to the fields to see if the rice seedlings needed watering. After Atu arrived at the fields, he looked at the short seedlings from left to right. He couldn't help but notice, "That's strange. These rice seedlings grow so slowly. It's been so many days now, and the seedlings have only grown a little bit. When will there be rice to harvest? This can't be right. I've got to think of a way to make them grow quicker!"

As he was saying that, he bent over and tried to slightly pull up one of the seedlings. Indeed, that particular seedling looked a little taller. Atu grew very excited. He stepped into the paddy to pull up every single seedling.

说著，他就蹲下身子，試著把一撮秧苗往上拉一點，果然，那秧苗看起來高了一些。

阿塗很興奮，立刻下田，把每一撮秧苗都拔高。

Atu busied himself with the seedlings all morning; he was exhausted! When he returned home, he lay down on the bed and exclaimed loudly, "I'm exhausted today!"

His father asked, "What did you do?"

Atu replied with pride, "I helped the rice seedlings grow taller!"

When his father heard this, he thought that it seemed rather odd. Not believing it was possible, his father asked Atu to take him to the fields to look.

忙了一上午，阿塗累極了！回到家，他往床上一躺，大聲說道：「今天我可累壞了！」

爸爸問：「怎麼了？」

阿塗很得意的說：「我幫秧苗長高了！」

爸爸聽了，覺得很奇怪，他不相信有這種事，便要阿塗帶他去田裏瞧瞧。

The two set out for the fields... Oh, no! All the rice seedlings had withered away and died! In disbelief, Atu stared with his eyes bulging wide open. He cried out, "How can it be! I..."

"What did you do?" angrily asked his father.

兩人到田裏一看,可不得了,所有的秧苗都枯死了!阿塗眼睛瞪得大大的,不敢相信的說:「怎麼會這樣!我⋯⋯」

爸爸很生氣的問他:「你是怎麼弄的?」

阿塗就把拔高秧苗的事告訴爸爸。爸爸搖搖頭，歎了口氣說：「你這傻孩子，你把秧苗拔高了，秧苗的根吸收不到營養和水分，當然會枯死！」

阿塗低下頭，很難為情的說：「爸爸，我錯了！以後我做事，再也不會那麼性急了！」

Atu told his father how he had pulled up all the rice seedlings. His father shook his head and sighed, "You foolish child. By pulling up the seedlings, the roots couldn't get any of the soil's nutrients or water. Naturally, they would wither and die!"

Lowering his head with embarrassment, Atu said, "Father, I was wrong! From now on, with everything that I do, I promise not to be impatient ever again!"

Parental Guide

From the above story, children learn that patience is needed to properly complete a task. However, in this competitive society, a great number of parents often unknowingly behave like Atu with his rice seedlings. Before children are ready physically and psychologically, some parents eagerly precipitate their children's learning. Because of the pressure to achieve in every field, children may react negatively. Children often show signs of stress, among other symptoms, when they have competitive parents. This story also reminds parents not to be overly demanding in our already competitive times. Furthermore, above story tells children that all things live according to certain principles. If we follow these principles and make adjustments for innovation, in time we'll attain success.

Chinese Children's Stories **series** consists of 100 volumes; 20 titles of subjects grouped in 5-book sets.

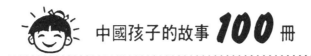 中國孩子的故事 **100** 冊

第①~⑤冊	中國民間故事	
第⑥~⑩冊	植物的故事	
第⑪~⑮冊	動物的故事	
第⑯~⑳冊	中國寓言故事	
第㉑~㉕冊	中國成語故事	
第㉖~㉚冊	節令的故事	
第㉛~㉟冊	食物的故事	
第㊱~㊵冊	發明的故事	
第㊶~㊺冊	十二生肖的故事	
第㊻~㊾冊	中國神仙故事	
第㊿~55冊	孝順的故事	
第56~60冊	中國奇童故事	
第61~65冊	中國神話故事	
第66~70冊	中國文學故事	
第71~75冊	中國名著故事	
第76~80冊	中國名人故事	
第81~85冊	中國歷史故事	
第86~90冊	中國地名故事	
第91~95冊	臺灣地名故事	
第96~100冊	臺灣民間故事	

First edition for the United States
published in 1991 by Wonder Kids Publications
Copyright © Emily Ching and Ko-Shee Ching 1991
Edited by Emily Ching, Ko-Shee Ching, and Dr. Theresa Austin
Chinese version first published 1988 by
Hwa-I Publishing Co.
Taipei, Taiwan, R.O.C.
All rights reserved.
All inquiries should be addressed to:
Wonder Kids Publications
P.O. Box 3485
Cerritos, CA 90703
International Standard Book No. 1-56162-024-6
Library of Congress Catalog Card No. 90-60796
Printed in Taiwan

MAIN LIBRARY

WITHDRAWN
FROM THE COLLECTION OF
WINDSOR PUBLIC LIBRARY